INNOCENCE AND EVIL

SHE WAS INNOCENT, BUT LONELINESS CHANGED HER FOREVER

ANUSHKA BANSAL

Made with ♥ on the Notion Press Platform
www.notionpress.com

Contents

CHAPTER ONE

THE MYTH

Centuries ago, there was a village located near Caldas, and not many people lived in the village, or shall we say that not many "sensible" people lived in the village. There weren't a lot of pretty people also, except for one exception.

The most beautiful girl that ever walked those streets was Sarah Ella Evans. All the girls would rack with jealousy, Sarah is who they wanted to be. The brunette with sparkling emerald eyes, and a perfect figure. Her angel voice could lure any man within a radius of 5 metres. Sarah was a perfect girl on the outside, and a kind one on the inside. But this didn't mean that she didn't have problems of her own, she had lost her mother in childbirth and her father blamed her for that till the day he died in a fire. The fire had been caused innocently by Sarah, but rumours spread that she caused it intentionally as she was tired of her old man.

She was shunned by her relatives as they all blamed her for killing her parents; she had few to no friends. There was a committee in the village where only a few selected people were, they were selected based on prettiness, smartness, richness, and legacy.

Soon after her father's death, Sarah was selected for the committee as she was considered the most pretty. There were people, people who had conflicts with Sarah. They believed that she was bad for whoever she got involved with, first her parents and now the people of the village. It was indeed a rumour; the village was filled with many of those, not to mention some scary myths.

One stood out in particular, they said that any girl who would see the blood moon would be cursed for the rest of her life, she would be left neither alive nor dead. The blood moon was indeed rare. Any person to see that moon and live through it was considered to be quite fortunate but the terror would stay with them forever and would drive them mad!

Like all things that happened to Sarah, the following event would be too; on a lonely winter night, the night of the blood moon, Sarah had gone out for a lovely stroll not knowing the status of the lunar cycle, she was the first girl in decades to see that moon, both eyes fixed upon it. That girl was not one to believe myths, especially when some of them included her, but what happened next would change her view forever.

Sarah returned home and didn't think much of it until the next day. It was at the crack of dawn when the poor girl woke up, she felt a bit weird but let it go, she went on with her day as usual but the night was one she would never forget.

As soon as she came out of her house and sparkled under the moonlight, her body changed. Her flesh disappeared like nothing, her bones started rattling and her insides were no longer there. She was shallow and empty.

A passing villager saw her and was frightened. He described it as "It was like Sarah disappeared. She looked like a demon which had come down to earth like somebody's skeleton came back from the grave."

The villagers thought of her as a witch and decided for her to burn at the stake. Sarah pleaded endlessly for her mercy, but none gave it to her. "I am just an innocent girl. Please! I beg you for mercy. Your soul will be blessed by God if you show mercy. Mercy!" begged Sarah, but the villagers didn't grant mercy. "Burn in hell for all eternity you wretched witch!" cried an old woman.

Sarah was burned at the stake, or that's what the people of the village thought. The curse didn't allow Sarah to die, it gave her immortality, but that gift was a curse to some, this included Sarah. She didn't have anyone and when she learned that she will be alone for all eternity, she drowned in her tears, her sorrow.

She decided not to frighten the villagers and to leave her home and go live in a faraway land. A land none knew of. She lived happily ever after, well at least for a while.....

CHAPTER TWO

PRETTY FACE, DARK SOUL

The year? Who remembered? The only thing Sarah could make out was the weather. It was the rainy season.

Sarah continued to live her sad, pathetic, boring, and lonely life which unfortunately could never end as a part of the curse placed on Sarah.

For the good of others, she remained isolated on a lonely deserted island. She couldn't help but wonder what she had turned into, only a few things stuck with her, the things that reminded her of her innocent childhood when everyone loved her and didn't have a worry in the world.

Some of the things that she could still do and that she loved were singing, something she was very excellent at one might say, and nothing.

There was no flora or fauna on the island, she couldn't do anything actually except sing.

Music was good for her. It connected her to the soul and it declared peace between the mind and the body.

One night singing in the rain with the rhythmic beats of falling clouds made her forget all the rusty roots that covered her. The oblivion refreshed her like a miracle overnight for which she had prayed to God from the days she opened her eyes to this reality realm. The tiny taps from her heels sided with the rock music of the thunders felt like something eventful and the lightning grooves snaking in the sky, from time to time, blacked out the running ruins in her veins that are waiting for the right time to flush her. She decided to cut all her connections to her past self

After all, why should she become a martyr when the rest of the world had already labelled her as a witch, a monster, someone dead, someone in the past who will not be remembered. Why care about those people who burned her to the stake without a thought or a doubt, why not thrive in becoming who she was now? Why be tortured endlessly till the end of times for people who have already forgotten her?

She decided to become the supposedly ruthless monster the world had made her out to be. A ruthless monster who pleasured the pain of others, the one who thrived on death and pain. The one who would be more hellish than Hades himself. Sarah wouldn't be the cutesy innocent small village girl anymore, she would be the creature sent from hell to walk the Earth destroying its every part. She would be evil inside-out, the more bloodshed there would be, the better.

Sarah figured out what she had been missing all along, it wasn't the need to live a nice life with luxury, it was for her to truly embrace what she was all along, what she had turned into. But nature being a big part of life, couldn't truly allow a creature this evil and shallow to walk the earth, to torment others while she lived happily in the pain of others.

Nature had to do something, and like everything this curse had a loophole too, even though Sarah couldn't die, she could be put into a long deep soundless sleep for years and years to come so the world could develop without such a monster ruining it. There was a big risk of someone finding the island one era or the other, so her bed had to be where no one could ever go.

The seabed of the Pacific, the deepest ocean there is. Thankfully, the island that monster lived on was surrounded by the Pacific. It was easy to put that creature to sleep.

One day, a huge earthquake came in the ocean, affecting Sarah's island too. She was naturally pushed into the ocean and as she didn't know the method to swim, she kept drowning and drowning, again and again, until she was on the sea bed in chains made of seaweed.

And thus, the ruthless monster was put to sleep in chains to never torment anyone ever again. Or so they thought. After all, every curse has a loophole.

CHAPTER THREE

AND THEN THERE WERE THREE

It had been more than a century since nature put Sarah to sleep. Apparently, a huge underwater earthquake was predicted to come in northwest America, where Sarah was asleep in the ocean.

The sudden earthquake caused tremendous ocean currents, causing the previous blood-thirsty monster's soul to return to Sarah's body.

She woke all of a sudden and took advantage of the earthquake to reach the surface. She was able to use the waves and go towards the island. After reaching there, she spotted a boat that had mysteriously appeared. She went exploring, taking a walk around the island in an attempt to find the people whose boat she saw and also hoping that she would get a nice feast out of their bodies after more than a century.

After a little walking, she saw two lovely boys, but one had a face and the clothes of the devil and the other looked like goody two shoes.

For the first time in her life, Sarah was concerned about her appearance. It looked like she wanted a good first impression of the boys. Sarah felt something she had never felt before. It was like her heart was smiling. Doubts arose, what was happening and what was the weird feeling? People called that weird feeling love but Sarah didn't know that as she had never felt love before. There were no pretty boys in the village where Sarah previously used to live.

Before Sarah could escape and wash her face with some ocean water, one of the boys spotted her and called her out "Hey gorgeous!"

Sarah froze not knowing what to do. She walked towards them. She stuttered. Sarah tried to make conversation but couldn't.

One of the boys introduced him as James and his older brother as Sebastian. Sarah told them her name and asked them when they arrived on the island. James answered it by saying a few days ago.

Over time, Sarah became more open to the boys and she loved talking to them.

On a fine day on a fine afternoon, Sarah was walking with James in search of wood while Sebastian was catching fish. They were going to eat fish for dinner; they hoped that Sebastian would catch a crab or a lobster which could be the centrepiece of the feast they were going to have.

While James was cutting a tree for more wood, Sarah began to talk with him trying to turn him against his brother. "Do you know James what happened last night? What Sebastian told me?" Sarah asked knowing that James does not know as no such thing happened. "Ummm....no? Why don't you tell me what Sebastian told you?" answered James with curiosity.

"Sebastian told me that he and you aren't really the best of brothers as you seem. He told me that in the past you let a girl come between you. He told me that her name was Ashley." Said Sarah. Sarah knew this all was true as she

had once overheard the brothers talking about Ashley.

James was shocked to hear this. He acted normal but he as a matter of fact was in surprise. Sarah caught this expression and gave an evil grin as she knew that her plan was in motion and was already proving to be successful. The walk back to Sebastian and where they had set camp was quite quiet. James was feeling more awkward with each step they took and finally had a sigh of relief when they reached the camp.

Sebastian was ready to cook the fishes he caught and he could tell something had happened. After dinner, Sarah went to sleep but James told Sebastian that he needed to talk about something important.

"Dear brother, after all that happened, I thought we were on good terms. I thought that we agreed never to bring the topic of Ash to life in the future", James said. Confused, Sebastian asked what he was talking about. "I thought that Ash was the past, we vowed never to look back and return to the darkest period of our life". Surprised, James told Sebastian what Sarah had said. It didn't take them long to figure out that Sarah was trying to break them

apart.

They were up all night figuring out why she was doing so. When the sun cracked a shine and Sarah woke up, they confronted her.

"You know our story, why would you still try to drive a wedge between us? This makes no sense Sarah, you pretended to be innocent but instead, you are the devil in the body of a peasant." cried James.

"Oh my god, do you really think you are the victim here? You couldn't be more wrong. You wouldn't believe what I've had to overcome. The voices in my head that won't let me rest, the demons that I've tried to suppress, the explosion of fireworks in my chest. I become more troubled as I try to calm the roaring noise inside my head. The panic surges and there are times when I am too petrified to lie with myself in the darkness to see what my body does next. I try to cover the violet stains from my sleepless nights. I hide it so well that you could never tell the journey I've been on, through hell and back. So, if you think that you are the victim here, you indeed are incorrect." said Sarah dramatically.

Upon hearing this, the brothers thought she was talking bluff. Well at least one of them thought so.

James understood her, he understood her pain, he could see the scars she tried to hide, after all, he was the good brother. "I am so sorry, I never understood your story till now, you don't deserve what I said to you, you don't deserve the life you live now. You deserve so much more. I vow to give you the life you so clearly deserve. The life where you don't have to live on a stranded island hoping that someday maybe your life will change for the better. Sarah Ella Evans, will you come to my town with me? A town where you can have a fresh start without any stains or blames from the past." asked James with his eyes full of hope.

THE DEPARTED

James stood there with his eyes so full of hope, hoping that Sarah would say yes, hoping that his heart won't be broken.

Sebastian on the other hand was shocked upon hearing this. He was shocked that his brother would betray him and betray the promises they made.

Sarah looked confused but happy at the same time.

"Yes! I will go with you for a fresh start at a new life." James screeched in happiness, he and Sarah, both were beyond happy but Sebastian was petrified. He hated Sarah for the things she did to him and his brother, he hated her for being so shallow. He hated his brother more for

the betrayal and the promises among them that were now all so clearly broken. He didn't utter a word to both of them for a few days.

James was devastated that his brother was sad and mad at him. Sarah didn't care that much about Sebastian, she only ever cared and thought about the life that she was now going to have.

After a few days, the time came for Sarah to once and for all leave the island behind along with her old life. James and Sarah were walking to their ship one final time.

They were walking close. Her left hand carried some flowers and the right one carried her luggage. James was carrying a few bags in each hand. They had rational lip movements, thinking about the same song. They walked in the same direction, here again, is a point to wonder, what on earth made their footsteps synchronised.

They reached the ship and departed happily. Their journey was long, Sebastian kept a log;

DAY 1

Today we started our journey. For some reason that witch named Sarah is coming with us, sorry let me correct that. Ahm. for some unknown but probably stupid reason, that witch known as Sarah is coming with my dear brother, James. They are also ignoring me as much as they can. I'd honestly rather die than handle this tormenting torture. Oh also another " great thing ", there may probably be a ninety-nine point nine percent chance of there being heavy rains tomorrow.

DAY 2

The rains today were terrific! We had to stay inside the ship rather than be sailing. I couldn 't stand Sarah and James!

DAY 4
Today Sarah and I had a faint conversation.

" What do you want, Sarah?"

"Peace, I want peace with you. I want to make a truce."

"Truce? After what you did. I will probably hold a grudge against you all my life."

"Sebastian, I've been in deep oceans before, but yours is making me drown."

"I don't care and I know that you don't care about my brother. It's all just an act."

"You have got me all wrong. He is the one thing that gets me up in the morning. He is the reason I am still breathing. He has given me the hope I've never got before. He cares more about me than anyone ever has. When I am with him, I forget all the pain, all the hurt, and all the bad. I truly cherish him and I always have, still, and always will love him. I promise you, I will not leave his heart broken."

"I hope so. He is an innocent roped into your madness."

*Hatred for her only started to grow for her
from here on...*

DAY 7

We hit a terrible turn...

DAY 15

I.
Hate.

My.

Stupid.

Life.

And.

I.

Wish.

To.

Disappear.

DAY 19

All my suicide attempts in the past three days have proven to be unsuccessful. Why do they even exist? Why do I even exist? Why does this whole damn world even exist? Sometimes I wonder if the world is just a game the gods are playing for fun and entertainment. If I am unfortunate, ill be back.

DAY 25

I wish this journey would end. I never believed that there could be a place worse than hell. I was so wrong. I wouldn't be surprised if Hades tossed me a pity look. I hate it so much that I wanna die or disappear and never return and to be buried in an unmarked grave or to be forgotten .

DAY 27

Enough is enough! I can't bear it any longer. I have decided to separate ways. I can't stand Sarah anymore. This journey may be long, but it's about to end for me.

DAY 30

Today was my last day on the ship, on the journey, and my last day of me talking to my brother. I am unfortunately in a foreign land, a land I never heard of until now. The people speak an unusual language, a language beyond my grasp. I am afraid I will starve and perish, I am afraid I won't be able to enjoy life again, the twists and turns of it. The good. The bad. All of it. I am afraid I won't be able to have any of it.

"

"

CHAPTER FIVE

BETRAYAL

The journey had ended. James was devastated. His brother had left him, abandoned him, whatever you consider. Sarah tried to console him numerous times but was unsuccessful each time.

"You make me happy, you make me smile

Break my heart a thousand times

I'll come back each time

They say 'Till Death do us Part'

Well they clearly don't know death

As cruel it may be,

Never so much

And never so daring To break two apart"

"You trying poetry now?" James said

"You tell me, is it good?" asked Sarah

"Nah" chuckled James

"Three whole days together,

And am like to love three more,

If it prove good weather."

"Sir John Suckling?

"You are familiar with his work?"

"Yeah, I am familiar with his work."

"Did you know that he died alone despite having numerous admirers?"

"I guess some people fall in love with the wrong people sometimes."

"I hope that doesn't happen to us."

"It won't, I won't let it."

"Promise me this is forever."

" I promise you."

"James, may I confess something, shift a burden off my shoulder?"

"Anything."

"I d-did something te-terrible."

"*What did you do?*"

"*I lied.*"

"*Who did you lie to?*"

"*The only person who ever loved me unconditionally, the only person who was ever kind to me. You. I lied to you and I lied horribly.*"

"*You. Lied. To. Me.*"

"*Yes.*"

"*What did you lie to me about?*"

"*About everything. About the truth. About my intentions, my feelings, about everything you know about me.*"

"*I beg your pardon.*"

"I am not the girl you think I am. I am just a selfish ruthless monster in whose plan you were just a minor who was manipulated and used as a means of escape. I never loved you, I was never capable of love."

"You lied to me, and for what? For a life that no version of you deserves? For a life led by lies and scandals.?"

"No! You don't get it, you don't know the pain I've been through. You only know the version of me I am right now, you don't know the beginning, you don't know the middle. You only know the end."

"Ok, so I don't know. Well I know this, you are a terrible person who should not be let to walk among commons and that you used me, drove a wedge between me and what I am now realising the only person who loves me and made us abandon each other."

"No no, there is time for you and your brother. You can look for him, I will even help you if you allow so, we will scavenge the entire world for Sebastian."

"No, we won't do anything. There is no we. There is only I and you."

"Ok. You know, we might have been. Maybe in another universe, we might have been. After all, they do say, 'Right person, wrong universe'."

"I have never heard anyone say that."

"Worth a shot. So is this goodbye then?"

"Goodbye Sarah. I hope to never cross paths with you in the future again."

"Don't be so harsh please, I had to do what I had to do. Goodbye."

Epilogue

After a search of many islands, the brothers James and Sebastian were finally able to reunite and they promised to never let anything drive them apart ever again. Sarah on the other hand decided to do something she never did, but always dreamed of doing. She decided to tour all of the world with tiny hopes in the bottom of her heart(if she has one) to find a cure for her monstrosity. Maybe the brothers and Sarah will cross paths again in the future, maybe they won't.